CLAUDIA BOLDT

YOU'RE A RUDE PIG, BERTIE!

YOU'RE A RUDE PIG, BERTIE!
A JONATHAN CAPE BOOK
978 1 780 08101 4

Published in Great Britain by Jonathan Cape,
an imprint of Random House Children's Publishers UK
A Random House Group Company
This edition published 2013

1 3 5 7 9 10 8 6 4 2

Copyright © Claudia Boldt, 2013

RANDOM HOUSE CHILDREN'S PUBLISHERS UK
61–63 Uxbridge Road, London W5 5SA

www.randomhousechildrens.co.uk
www.randomhouse.co.uk

Addresses for companies within The Random House Group Limited can
be found at: www.randomhouse.co.uk/offices.htm
THE RANDOM HOUSE GROUP Limited Reg. No. 954009
A CIP catalogue record for this book is available from the British Library.
Printed in China

To Simon, Luis and Kio

CLaudia BOLDT

YOU'RE a RUDE PIG, BERTIE!

Jonathan Cape · London

Bertie was a most unpleasant pig. He thought of no one but himself.

Every morning he looked in the mirror and said, "Who is the most beautiful piglet in the world? It is me, myself and I – wonderful Monsieur Pig – Bertie the Pig!"

Bertie always had something nasty to say about everyone he met.

"Dreadful hair today, Mrs Harley!"

"Without your annoying husband, Mrs Block?"

"Long time no see, Mrs Breun.
You look older!"

"Joseph! Your bad smell never ceases to amaze me!"

It was no wonder that Bertie had no friends.

But one day Bertie met Ruby. She was the cutest
rabbit he had ever seen and to Bertie's surprise
he found himself saying, "Your ears are so long.
How extraordinarily beautiful!"

Ruby was very flattered and gave him
an extra big piece of cheese.

Chèvre
Feta
Edam
Gouda
Leerdammer
Shropshire Blue
Muenster Cheese

Cheese
Ch... ay
Hal...umi
Dan... lue
Chee...
Egg...
Bonifa...

Ram
Ram
Ram
Ram

On the way home, Bertie bumped into Roland the sausage dog, who could not believe his ears when Bertie said, "What a lovely day! And look at you, you are looking splendid!"

All day he could think of nothing but Ruby
and how nice she was.

Bertie decided to impress her
by throwing a huge party.

TO
ARNOLD
THE UGLY

Hello loser, I am having a party. Best, B.

Hildegard! I know it-all, I wasn't going to invite you but come anyway.

Dear mayor, I don't like you but I invite you anyway.

If she came he would even show her
his big collection of marble eggs.
Nothing seemed to be too great an effort.

Bertie's invitations were sent out and the party was the talk of the town. But Ruby was not impressed that Bertie had insulted all of her friends. In fact everyone had had enough of him and his rudeness.

THESE ARE JUST a FEW OF THE DISHES BERTIE PREPARED.

It was the day of the party and at three o'clock everything was prepared. But no one came. Bertie was disappointed. "Where is everyone? Did they not receive their invitations? Doesn't Ruby like me?"

Bertie went to bed early after his miserable day.

Bertie woke up all sweaty and upset. "The toothbrush is right! This is terrible . . . Is this why no one has come to my party?"

Bertie wanted to to get some fresh
air to forget about his nightmare,
so he went for a walk.

There was Hildegard. "Hey,
Hildegard! I . . ." But she had
already turned her back on him.

Then he saw Mrs Harley and said:
"Hello!" But she did not even grace
him with a look in return.

Then Bertie heard Arnold
whispering: "That pig is so rude.
He will never have any friends."

Bertie was very sad and decided that some cheese would cheer him up. He queued up next to Mr Wolf.

Mr Wolf was annoyed that he had to wait and grumbled: "Hurry up! Can't you hear me? What are these silly long ears good for anyway? If . . ."

He could not finish his sentence because Bertie
grunted very loudly: "Don't speak to Ruby like that!"

"That was nice, Bertie," said Ruby.
Bertie blushed and said,
"Really?! Thank you!"

People smiled at Bertie,
and Arnold even nodded
his approval.

Finally Bertie knew what to do . . .

This time everyone came, apart from
Mrs Harley who still held a grudge.
But most important of all, Ruby was there
and it was the best party ever!